Immortals

HERO

Pirate Queen

Steve Barlow and Steve Skidmore

Illustrated by Judit Tondora

Franklin Watts
First published in Great Britain in 2019 by The Watts Publishing Group

Text © Steve Barlow and Steve Skidmore 2019
Illustrations by Judit Tondora © Franklin Watts 2019
The "2Steves" illustration by Paul Davidson
used by kind permission of Orchard Books

PB ISBN 978 1 4451 6954 5
ebook ISBN 978 1 4451 6955 2
Library ebook ISBN 978 1 4451 6956 9

1 3 5 7 9 10 8 6 4 2

Printed in Great Britain

Franklin Watts
An imprint of
Hachette Children's Group
Part of The Watts Publishing Group
Carmelite House
50 Victoria Embankment
London EC4Y 0DZ

An Hachette UK Company
www.hachette.co.uk

www.franklinwatts.co.uk

How to be a hero

This book is not like others you have read. This is a choose-your-own-destiny book where YOU are the hero of this adventure.

Each section of this book is numbered. At the end of most sections, you will have to make a choice. Each choice will take you to a different section of the book.

If you choose correctly, you will succeed. But be careful. If you make a bad choice, you may have to start the adventure again. If this happens, make sure you learn from your mistake!

Go to the next page to start your adventure. And remember, don't be a zero, be a hero!

It is the year 1705.

Your father is chief of the Tortuga Brethren, the greatest company of pirates in the Caribbean. He has sent you to England to be educated.

You have finished your schooling at Miss Rosetta Stone's Academy for Young Gentlewomen, and today you have just beaten your fencing instructor, Marcel, for the first time.

"Mademoiselle, I have nothing more to teach you."

A housemaid comes in to announce that Miss Stone wants to see you.

Go to 1.

1

"There you are!" says Miss Stone. "This is Captain Jenkins. He has a message for you."

Jenkins bows. "A rival pirate, Redhand Radcliff, is challenging your father's position as leader of the Tortuga Brethren.

"Under your father, our ships rob the enemies of England and its good Queen Anne of their ill-gotten treasure and precious cargo, but we always spare the crew. Radcliff does not. His motto is *No witnesses*.

"Your father has heard that Redhand plans to kidnap you in the hope it will force him to give up his position as leader. Then Redhand will take control of the Brethren. If you wish, I will take you to your father, on my ship the *Happy Wanderer*."

Miss Stone gives you a meaningful look. "I'd like a word, if you please."

If you don't want to go, go to 24.
To hear what Miss Stone has to say, go to 37.

2

"Bring your men aboard," you order.

As the last of the stricken vessel's crew take to the boats, it sinks beneath the waves.

You have saved your father's men — but what should you do about the treasure ship they tried to capture?

To take news of the treasure ship to your father, go to 40.

To go after the treasure ship yourself, go to 7.

3

"Set a course southwest. If we hold steady at seven knots, we should arrive at Tortuga in good time," you order.

The pirates cheer. "She knows how to navigate!" cries Ned. "She's her father's daughter. Will you have her as captain?"

The pirates roar, "Aye!"

You appoint Ned your first mate, thanking your stars that you spent every summer holiday in England learning how to sail with a retired friend of your father's, now a respectable smuggler in the West Country.

Next day, at dawn, the lookout reports an unknown ship nearby.

"What is she?" you ask. "Merchantman? Royal Navy? Another pirate?"

"I can't tell," comes the reply.

To order your men to fire on the ship, go to 22.

To sail alongside it, go to 26.

4

You chase the treasure ship, but soon
realise that the closer ship is bigger than
the *Happy Wanderer*. It is flying the pirate
flag, the skull and crossbones.

Ned groans. "I know that ship. It's the
Barracuda. Its captain is Redhand Radcliff,
your father's greatest enemy."

The vessel shows a white flag. A figure
on the foredeck wearing a red frock coat
and tricorn hat cries, "Parley!" He wants to
speak with you under the pirate code.

To ignore this call, go to 23.
To speak to Radcliff, go to 49.
To fire on the *Barracuda*, go to 15.

5

You point towards the treasure ship.

"Enough talking! She's getting away!"

Your ship and the *Barracuda* separate to chase down the treasure ship. Redhand's vessel, being faster, soon pulls ahead. You wonder if Redhand wishes to take the ship for himself?

To signal Redhand to slow down, go to 27.

To fire on the *Barracuda*, go to 15.

To watch and wait, go to 36.

6

The moment you set foot on Jenkins's ship, the *Happy Wanderer*, you sense that all is not well. The crew are sullen and watchful.

As the men tend the sails and the vessel starts to move, an old sailor takes your arm.

"Ned Dawkins, miss," he whispers. "Cap'n Jenkins is a traitor — he's in Redhand's pay. But there are still plenty of men on board loyal to your father. With you to lead us, we'll rise up and take the ship! Just say the word!"

Miss Stone was right, you think.

To accept Ned's offer, go to 17.
To wait and see what Jenkins intends to do, go to 32.

7

With the rescued men's help, you set a course to follow the treasure ship.

Ned comes to see you in your cabin. "You made the right decision, Captain," he says. "Your father wants that treasure to help England in her war with Spain. He's hoping for a pardon from Queen Anne so he can return to land safely. He says an old pirate who doesn't retire must rest his bones with Davy Jones if you take my meaning..."

One of the crew bursts in.

"Captain," he cries, "the lookout says the treasure ship is in sight — but there's a storm a'comin', and it looks a bad one. What are your orders?"

Strong winds may tear the sails to ribbons, and damage the masts — but if you take in sail and slow down now, you may lose the treasure ship.

To give the order to take in sail, go to 35.

To risk leaving the sails up, go to 43.

8

As soon as the exchange is complete, Redhand roars with laughter and orders his crew to seize your men.

At the same moment, the men Redhand has sent you as "hostages" produce concealed weapons and attack! Your crew, taken by surprise, are helpless. Redhand's men rush at you, swords raised to chop you to bits!

Go to 28.

9

"I can't have him aboard," you say. "His men may try to free him. Cast him adrift in an open boat."

Some of Jenkins's men grumble at this, but you are within your rights according to the pirate code. Jenkins will have food and water, charts and a compass. If he is brave and lucky, he will survive.

Once the *Happy Wanderer* is under
way again, you must decide what to do
about the men you believe are still loyal
to Jenkins.

To lock them up, go to 14.
To try to win them over, go to 34.

10

The Navy ship is too fast for you to escape. You order your crew to give battle.

You fight courageously, but your men are no match for the highly-trained and disciplined gunners of the Navy. The *Happy Wanderer* is being shot to pieces all around you. There is only one way of escape.

Go to 28.

11

"We mustn't lose the treasure ship!" you cry. "Hold your course!"

Next minute, your ship is struck by a monstrous wave. Sails are blown away, masts reduced to splinters. Unable to steer, you can only watch helplessly as the ship turns sideways to the waves. The *Happy Wanderer* is doomed. There is only one way of escape.

Go to 28.

12

You order your helmsman to steer straight for the treasure ship. As the vessels collide, your men stream on to her from one side as Redhand's crew board from the other. The fighting is soon over, and the treasure ship's crew under guard.

You meet Redhand on the quarterdeck.

"Time to divide the treasure," you say. "Half and half, as agreed."

Redhand gives you an evil grin. "Oh, no, missy. My ship engaged the enemy first. That makes the treasure mine!"

To order your crew to fight Redhand's men, go to 39.

To challenge Redhand to single combat, go to 29.

13

You book passage on a merchantman. But two days out from port, your ship is stopped by a vessel flying the pirate flag: the skull and crossbones!

The captain of the pirate ship is Redhand Radcliff! He looks at you inquisitively. "And who might this be?" He turns to the captain of the merchantman. "Tell me or it will go badly for you!"

The captain tells Redhand who you are.

"Well, well, if it ain't the very person I've been looking for!" He moves towards you with his sword raised. There's only one way out of this!

Go to 28.

14

"Put them in irons," you order.

Jenkins's men seem to accept their fate. Your crew lead them down into the hold.

But at night, the prisoners break loose! Surprise is on their side and, after fierce hand-to-hand fighting, they once more gain control of the ship.

Their new leader, a dirty ruffian with many scars, leers at you. "Chop her into cat's meat, boys!"

Your friends among the crew are powerless. There is only one way to escape.

Go to 28.

15

"Run out the guns!" you order. "Fire!"

But Redhand's reply is immediate. The *Barracuda*'s guns roar, and you quickly realise that your opponent's ship is much more heavily armed than yours. Cannonballs rip your sails and rigging to pieces, and tear through the hull. You can only watch helplessly as the treasure ship escapes and the *Happy Wanderer* sinks beneath your feet. There is only one way to survive.

Go to 28.

16

Ruthlessly, you sail away from the sinking ship.

As it disappears beneath the waves, your crew mutter angrily. The pirate code says that any fellow pirate in trouble should be offered help. Before you can act to restore order, some of the hotheads among your crew seize you and drag you to the ship's rail.

"You've drowned those poor souls: sent them down to Davy Jones," snarls one, "and now you can go with them!"

Go to 28.

17

"You know who to trust," you tell Ned. "Make your plans — we strike tonight!"

At midnight, Ned fetches you from your cabin. Those crew men still loyal to your father are already fighting Jenkins's men. You jump straight into the fray, displaying your impressive sword skills.

Soon, cries of triumph ring out. The *Happy Wanderer* is yours!

Jenkins is brought before you. "What shall we do with him?" demands Ned.

To order your men to throw Jenkins overboard, go to 45.

To spare Jenkins, go to 9.

18

You fire a warning shot.

Redhand takes this as an offensive move against the *Barracuda*, and turns to attack. His blazing guns soon reduce the *Happy Wanderer* to matchwood. As she begins to sink, you take the only possible way of escape.

Go to 28.

19

Taking heed of Miss Stone's warning, you leave the academy and head for the London docks. You find the *Happy Wanderer* and wonder what to do.

To go on board Jenkins's ship, go to 6.
To find another ship heading for Tortuga, go to 13.

20

Ignoring Ned's protests, you take a boat across to the *Barracuda*.

Redhand invites you to his cabin, where

he opens a box of sweets.

"Marzipan," he says. "Take one."

You haven't eaten sweets since you left Miss Stone's academy. Greedily, you stuff one into your mouth. You immediately feel sick and woozy.

Redhand laughs. "Knockout drops!" he says. "I'll take your ship without firing a shot!"

Go to 28.

21

Running before the wind, the *Happy Wanderer* escapes the worst of the storm.

At daybreak, the weather calms and the lookout reports the sails of two ships in view: one is the treasure ship, but the other ship is closer.

To order your crew to chase the treasure ship, go to 4.

To investigate the new ship, go to 47.

22

"We can't take chances," you say. "Open fire!"

"Aye-aye, Cap'n," says Ned. "Where should we aim? For the sails, or for the hull?"

To aim for the ship's sails, go to 30.

To aim at her hull, go to 38.

23

"Parley denied!" you yell back, and order more sail.

But the *Barracuda* easily overhauls you, and fires a broadside. Cannonballs tear your sails and rigging to pieces. Soon two of your masts are down and your hull is wrecked.

"I surrender!" you cry.

Redhand laughs mercilessly. "No witnesses!"

You realise there is only one way of escape.

Go to 28.

"I have no wish to live among pirates. I will not go to Tortuga," you tell Jenkins.

Miss Stone looks disappointed. "I think you should reconsider," she says. "What I have to tell you is very important."

"Very well," you reply. "I will listen to what you have to say."

Go to 37.

25

"I don't need hostages," you tell Redhand, adding untruthfully, "I trust your word."

"Very well," replies Redhand. "But when we take the treasure ship, its crew must be fed to the sharks. No witnesses!"

To avoid giving an answer, go to 5.
To agree to Redhand's terms, go to 41.

26

The strange ship is badly damaged. The hull has been smashed by cannon-shot, the sails are in rags. It is eerily silent. There don't seem to be enough men on board to sail her.

You steer to within hailing distance.

"What ship is that?" you cry.

"One of the Tortuga Brethren," comes the reply. "We found a Spanish treasure ship carrying lots of gold and weapons to the South American colonies at war with England. We fought her, but she was too strong for us!"

The damaged ship may be one of your father's, but you see it can't remain afloat much longer.

To abandon the ship and its crew to their fate, go to 16.

To invite the ship's crew to join you, go to 2.

27

You fly signal flags ordering Redhand to slow down. He ignores them. Should you just attack him now or give him a chance and fire a warning shot?

To fire a warning shot across the *Barracuda*'s bows, go to 18.

To attack the *Barracuda*, go to 15.

To wait and see what Redhand does, go to 36.

28

You grip the Eye of the Sea and cry, "Lord Neptune, save me!"

With a great crashing of waves and a burst of light, you find yourself, unharmed, back in Miss Stone's study.

"I see you have discovered how treacherous the pirate world can be," she says drily. "Begin your voyage again — but choose more wisely this time!"

Go to 19.

Redhand sneers, but cannot refuse with his men looking on. You both raise your swords and set to.

Redhand is a stronger swordsman, but thanks to your lessons with Marcel you are more nimble and faster. Soon, you send Redhand's sword flying from his hand.

The pirate code says that Redhand's crew must now accept you as their new captain. Losing their fear of their defeated leader, they seize him eagerly. "Shall we feed him to the fishes, Cap'n?" asks Ned.

You shake your head. "No — we're not like him. We'll maroon him on a desert island. We can always pick him up later — if anyone can be bothered!"

Go to 50.

30

"Aim for the sails," you order. If you can damage its sails and rigging badly enough, the ship will be at your mercy.

The *Happy Wanderer*'s cannons fire with an ear-splitting roar. Holes appear in the ship's sails. Distant figures run about the decks, waving their arms. A white flag is hauled up to the masthead. The stranger has surrendered.

To continue firing, go to 38.
To go alongside the stranger, go to 26.

31

"No thanks!" you call.

Redhand laughs. "Then let's exchange hostages — as a promise of good behaviour!"

You consider this. If you hold some of Redhand's men prisoner, he can't betray you without putting them at risk. But it means placing your men at Redhand's mercy.

To agree to exchange hostages, go to 8.
To refuse, go to 25.

32

"I will give you my answer tonight," you tell Ned. He looks disappointed, but nods and moves away.

Over the course of the day, you decide that you cannot trust Jenkins — you will have to fight for your freedom!

As you look for Ned to tell him of your decision, you are seized from behind. Jenkins appears. "My men tell me you are plotting mutiny," he says. "The penalty for that is death."

As he reaches for a pistol, you realise there is only one way of escape.

Go to 28.

33

Your final broadside sinks the treasure ship.

Seeing that the treasure is lost, Redhand turns his fury on you. The *Barracuda*'s heavy guns soon reduce the *Happy Wanderer* to a burning wreck.

Go to 28.

34

You face Jenkins's men boldly. "You know my father," you say. "He's a leader of men, and so am I. Make me your captain. I will lead you to plunder and good fortune!"

One of Jenkins's crew unrolls a chart.

"I marked our position before your men took the ship," he says. "So tell me, 'Cap'n', what course do we take for Tortuga?"

You must make the right decision or you will never earn the respect of these men. You look carefully at the chart.

To steer east, go to 46.
To steer southwest, go to 3.

Your instinct is to stay close to the treasure ship — but you can't do that if you lose your masts to the storm. At your order, men climb into the rigging to take in sail.

The treasure ship draws ahead. As the storm thickens, you lose sight of it.

When the storm has passed, the lookout spots a sail. You order your men to pursue the ship.

You realise your mistake when the ship hoists the White Ensign. It's not the treasure ship; it's a Royal Navy man-o'-war!

Go to 10.

36

Ned clenches his fists. "Redhand will reach the treasure first!"

"Wait," you tell him.

The *Barracuda* catches the treasure ship and opens fire.

"He'll not wait for us," says Ned grimly. "Orders, Cap'n?"

To order an attack on the *Barracuda*, go to 48.

To attack the treasure ship on the other side, go to 44.

37

Miss Stone points to the door.

"Captain Jenkins, leave us a moment."

When Jenkins has left the room, Miss Stone takes your hand. "You must help your father. He is a good man, and Redhand Radcliff is a monster!"

You stare at her. "What do you know of my father?"

She laughs. "These days, I am Miss Rosetta Stone, schoolmistress." Her voice hardens. "But once, I was Swordfish Sal, terror of the Spanish Main and a friend of your father. I know he would not ask you to go to him without good reason. You must do as he asks…"

"Very well," you reply. "I will go."

Go to 42.

38

"Fire at the hull!" you order, but your shipmates raise a howl of protest.

"You can't just sink her!" growls one.

"Aye!" says another. "She could have treasure — and what use is treasure in the sea?"

You don't yet know enough about pirate ways and say, "Men, if you're willing to take the risk, so am I! Lay us alongside!"

Go to 26.

39

"If you want the treasure," you say grimly, "you'll have to fight for it!"

As your men and Redhand's fight, the crew of the treasure ship take advantage of the confusion to overcome their guards. They attack and retake the ship. Their captain gestures with his sword.

"Throw the pirate dogs overboard!"

As you fall towards the shark-infested waters, you have one chance of survival.

Go to 28.

40

You set a course for Tortuga to bring news of the treasure ship to your father. Before long, the lookout spots another sail.

As you get closer, you see that the ship is flying the White Ensign. It's a Royal Navy ship, running down on you with the wind in its favour. And the Navy has sworn to destroy all pirates...

Go to 10.

41

"I accept!" you cry.

But your men are angry. "'Tis against the pirate code to kill prisoners," one yells.

"Aye," another agrees. "You're as treacherous as Redhand himself! If blood's to be shed, we'll start with yours!"

Your furious crew advance on you, swords held ready to strike.

Go to 28.

40—41

Miss Stone opens a drawer of her desk and takes out a pendant. From its golden chain hangs a strange jewel.

"This is the Eye of the Sea. It holds great power. If you are in deadly danger, grasp it and cry, 'Lord Neptune, save me!', and you will find yourself back in this time and place."

You thank Miss Stone and take the jewel.

"One more thing," says Miss Stone. "Be careful of Jenkins. I've heard he'd sell his soul to the highest bidder."

Go to 19.

43

Fearful of losing the treasure ship, you decide to crack on under full sail. But the storm is more ferocious than you expected. Soon, waves are crashing over the deck.

"We must run before the storm," Ned yells over the wind, "or we're done for!"

Ned is right: the ship has a much better chance of riding out the storm with the wind behind her. But if you change course, you may lose the treasure ship.

If you want to hold your course, go to 11.

To follow Ned's advice, go to 21.

44

Battered by fire from two ships at once, the treasure ship is in danger of sinking; but still, her captain refuses to surrender.

To order your men to board the treasure ship, go to 12.

To continue firing on her, go to 33.

45

"He is a traitor," you say harshly. "Feed him to the sharks!"

As your men hesitate to carry out this cruel order, Jenkins's crew rush to their captain's defence. Fighting breaks out again, and this time your enemies are victorious.

Jenkins glares at you. "She's caused enough trouble," he rages. "Show her no mercy!"

His men bear down on you, swords raised and grinning horribly.

Go to 28.

46

"Steer to the east!" you say.

"Hear that, comrades?" cries Jenkins's shipmate as the crew laugh. "She'll take us back to London, and see us all hanged as pirates, every mother's son!"

You realise your mistake. "I meant southw-w-west," you stammer.

But it is too late. All the pirates charge you with blood-curdling cries!

Go to 28.

47

You point to the new sail. "Let's see what ship that is. It may be my father's."

But as you approach the new sail, the lookout gives a cry of terror. "That's the *Barracuda* — Redhand Radcliff's ship!"

You give orders to turn tail and run — but too late! Redhand's ship opens fire, and a lucky shot brings down your mainmast. You are helpless beneath your enemy's guns! As the *Barracuda*'s cannon smash your hull like matchwood, you take the only possible way to escape.

Go to 28.

48

"Take us alongside the *Barracuda*," you say. "We'll attack while they're too busy to defend her."

But as soon as you open fire, you realise your mistake. The *Barracuda* is heavily armed, and has enough men to fight on both sides of the ship at once.

The *Barracuda*'s fire is merciless and you soon feel the *Happy Wanderer* begin to sink under you.

Go to 28.

49

"What do you want?" you shout.

"An alliance!" roars Redhand. "Half the treasure each when we take the galleon!"

You don't trust Redhand, but if you fight him, the treasure ship will get away.

"Come aboard!" cries Redhand.

To accept, go to 20.

To refuse, go to 31.

50

When you sail into Tortuga, you are captain of three ships — the *Happy Wanderer*, the *Barracuda* and the Spanish treasure ship.

Your father is delighted with your success.

"When I sent for you," he says, "it wasn't just to keep you safe from Redhand Radcliff. I wanted to prepare you to take over as chief of the Brethren when I retire. But," he adds, "you seem to have done all your preparation on the way. You've arrived here a hero!"

He takes off his hat and places it on your head as the Tortuga Brethren enthusiastically welcome their new Pirate Queen.

I HERO Quiz

Test yourself with this special quiz. It has been designed to see how much you remember about the book you've just read. Can you get all five answers right?

Question 1

Where are you at the start of this sea adventure?

A   on board the ship

B   at the docks

C   at Miss Rosetta Stone's Academy for Young Gentlewomen

D   Tortuga

Question 2

What was Miss Rosetta Stone's pirate name?

A   Deadly Drake

B   Captain Candice

C   The Sailing Lady

D   Swordfish Sal

Question 3

What does Miss Rosetta Stone give the Pirate Queen?

A   a strange jewel

B   an ancient pirate sword

C   a parrot

D   a diamond-encrusted dagger

Question 4

What is your mission as the Pirate Queen?

A   capture Miss Rosetta Stone

B   kill your father

C   steal Redhand's hat

D   stop Redhand Radcliff

Question 5

What does Redhand Radcliff want?

A   kidnap you, the Pirate Queen

B   destroy Miss Rosetta's academy

C   steal an ancient treasure map

D   become a schoolteacher

About the 2Steves

"The 2Steves" are
one of Britain's
most popular writing
double acts for young
people, specialising
in comedy and
adventure. They

perform regularly in schools and libraries,
and at festivals, taking the power of words
and story to audiences of all ages.

Together they have written many books,
including the *Monster Hunter* series.
Find out what they've been up to at:
www.the2steves.net

About the illustrator: Judit Tondora

Judit Tondora was born in Miskolc, Hungary
and now works from her countryside studio.
Judit's artwork has appeared in books, comics,
posters and on commercial design projects.

To find out more about her work, visit:
**www.astound.us/publishing/artists/
judit-tondora**

Have you completed these I HERO adventures?

Battle with monsters in Monster Hunter:

978 1 4451 5878 5 pb	978 1 4451 5935 5 pb	978 1 4451 5936 2 pb	978 1 4451 5939 3 pb
978 1 4451 5876 1 ebook	978 1 4451 5933 1 ebook	978 1 4451 5937 9 ebook	978 1 4451 5940 9 ebook

978 1 4451 5942 3 pb
978 1 4451 5943 0 ebook

978 1 4451 5945 4 pb
978 1 4451 5946 1 ebook

Defeat all the baddies in Toons:

978 1 4451 5930 0 pb	978 1 4451 5921 8 pb	978 1 4451 5924 9 pb	978 1 4451 5918 8 pb
978 1 4451 5931 7 ebook	978 1 4451 5922 5 ebook	978 1 4451 5925 6 ebook	978 1 4451 5919 5 ebook

Also by the 2Steves...

978 1 4451 5985 0

GALAXY WARRIORS
GALAXY FOOTBALL CUP
STEVE BARLOW ❖ STEVE SKIDMORE
SANTY GUTIERREZ

Tip can't believe his luck when he mysteriously wins tickets to see his favourite team in the cup final. But there's a surprise in store ...

978 1 4451 5892 1

GALAXY WARRIORS
SPACE CHASE
STEVE BARLOW ❖ STEVE SKIDMORE
SANTY GUTIERREZ

Big baddie Mr Butt Hedd is in hot pursuit of the space cadets and has tracked them down for Lord Evil. But can Jet, Tip and Boo Hoo find a way to escape in a cunning disguise?

978 1 4451 5988 1

GALAXY WARRIORS
SPACE PIRATES

Jet and Tip get a new command from Master Control to intercept some precious cargo. It's time to become space pirates!

978 1 4451 5979 9

GALAXY WARRIORS
WEB WORLD
STEVE BARLOW ❖ STEVE SKIDMORE
SANTY GUTIERREZ

The goodies intercept a distress signal and race to the rescue. Then some 8-legged fiends appear ... Tip and Jet realise it's a trap!